I Want My Dinner

Tony Ross

Andersen Press · London

"I WANT MY DINNER!"

"Say PLEASE," said the Queen.

"I want my dinner . . . please."

"Mmmmm, lovely."

"I want my potty."

"Say PLEASE," said the General.

"I want my potty, PLEASE."

"Mmmmm, lovely."

"I want my Teddy . . .

. . . PLEASE," said the Princess.

"Mmmmm."

"We want to go for a walk . . . PLEASE."

"Mmmmm."

"Mmmmm . . . that looks good."

"HEY!" said the Beastie.

"That's MY dinner."

"I want my dinner!"

"Say PLEASE," said the Princess.

"I want my dinner, PLEASE."

"Mmmmm."

"HEY!" said the Princess.

"Say THANK YOU."

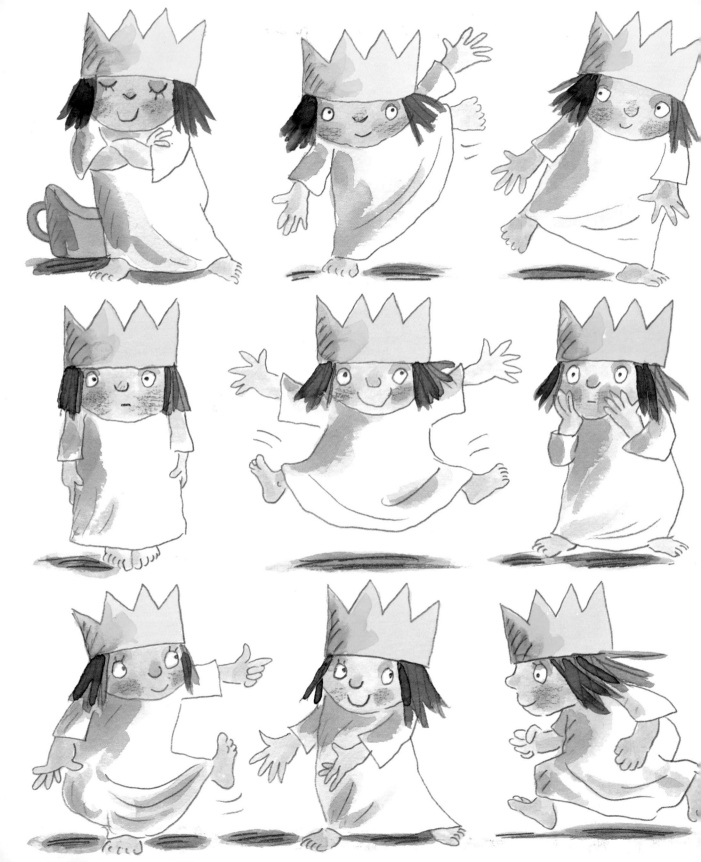